A Road Once Travelled

E. Randolph Underwood

A Road Once Travelled

ISBN: 9781070628622
Independently Published

DEDICATION

This novella is dedicated to all of the people who have provided the guidance, help, and encouragement that have paved the road I've travelled through a long and successful journey through life.

A Road Once Travelled .

CONTENTS

A Road Once Travelled

ACKNOWLEDGMENTS

I would like to express a special thank you to my wife, Cathy, for her encouragement during this and my other writing endeavors. Without your patience and support, I would not be able to fulfill this dream.

I would also like to acknowledge and thank Jerry Juliana, Joe Underwood, and Bruce Waldron for their reviews, comments, and valuable suggestions throughout the writing process.

A Road Once Travelled

CHAPTER 1

It was 5:30 a.m. in Houston, Texas, and Ron Samuels was sitting at his kitchen table wondering about his future. He had been a special projects engineer for a major oil company until the company had retired and ungraciously escorted him and four other "old hands" from the building the previous day with their personal belongings and a severance package the company had deemed generous.

The reason given for their release from the company was the need to downsize to accommodate changing market conditions. So much for twenty-seven years of loyal service, sacrifice, and millions of dollars he had saved them with prevented accidents, uninterrupted production, and innovative solutions around the world.

Ron should have retired three years before when he was sixty-two. He and his wife, Fran, had planned to take early retirement, buy a motor home, and spend the next twenty to twenty-five years going places and doing things they had never had the time for during their busy careers. Those plans had ended when he allowed the company to talk him into taking a two-year overseas assignment to manage a major environmental project. Unfortunately, fate had stepped in and Fran had died from a rare infection while they were overseas.

Ron returned to Houston after Fran's death, buried himself in his work, and put retirement plans on indefinite hold. Somehow, he hadn't seen the changes occurring around him and the signs that he and some of the other "dinosaurs" in the company were being viewed as part of the outdated office furniture and equipment. Maybe it was time to pass the torch to the younger generation who had grown up with the technology and culture that had fueled the changes, but the way he and his friends had been let go still cut him to the core.

The gravity of the events of the previous day was finally settling in as he sat there drinking his coffee and coming to the realization that he was alone with no place to go and nothing to do. What was he going to do with the new-found freedom, time, and money that had suddenly dropped into his lap?

The last time he had felt this alone and uncertain of his future had been a night in early June, 1964, as he rode a train into West Virginia to spend the summer with an aunt and uncle he barely knew. He was a fourteen-year-old boy from inter-city Baltimore who was being involuntarily exiled to the sticks away from his friends and familiar surroundings. His parents could just as well have sent him to Siberia. What was the difference?

His parents had a good reason for sending him out of the city. He had started running with the wrong crowd and had gotten himself into some minor legal trouble. More significantly, he had developed a world class attitude and a strong allergy to any kind of productive endeavor. Charity, or perhaps the impatience of his teachers, had been the only reason he had been promoted from the eighth to the ninth grade. Young Ronald James Samuels was in essence a disaster waiting for a time and place to happen.

His parents had given up trying to reform him. Both had to work outside the home to make ends meet and the young man just slipped out and did whatever he wanted to do while they weren't home. Their last hope was to send him to Jenny and Fred Striver, his hard-nosed school teacher aunt and her former drill sergeant husband, in hopes that they could do something with him. The couple had accepted the challenge and the young man, their reclamation project for the summer, found himself on a train to West Virginia.

As Ron sat in his kitchen thinking about that long-ago summer, he felt a sudden longing to return to West Virginia and travel again some of the roads he had travelled while there. He had no idea why he was being drawn back there, nor what he might find. Aunt Jenny and Uncle Fred had both been dead for years and Ron no longer had family ties there. There was, however, an unexplainable bond he had developed with the place during that long-ago summer that was bidding him to come back.

He mulled the idea through his mind and decided the trip might do him some good. He definitely had the time and money to do it. The only concern was the possibility of being disappointed with what he might find. That was certainly a possibility given the passage of more than half a century, but he couldn't let that stop him. He needed to get out of Houston for awhile, and he had to do it as soon as possible.

Within an hour, Ron had booked a flight to Pittsburgh the following Monday morning, a return flight on Friday afternoon, and reservations for a rental car and a motel near Clarksburg, the closest town with overnight accommodations. That would give him three full days to drive around, explore, and reminisce. All he could do then was to be at the Houston airport Monday at 10:00 a.m. and the Pittsburgh airport Friday at 12:35 p.m. Beyond that, he'd just have to follow his memories and emotions to see where they would lead.

He spent Sunday evening struggling with what to pack. Remembering that people in West Virginia were down to earth country people who didn't cater to a lot of formality, he decided to pack nothing but casual and comfortable clothing that would fit in a carry-on bag. That was topped off with a light jacket, rain parka, and waterproof hat that fit nicely into the small backpack he could carry in the car during his daily jaunts into the countryside. Anything else could be picked up and then left behind when he returned home.

The objective, plan, and logistics were in place. All he had to do was to execute the plan and accomplish his first post-retirement mission.

CHAPTER 2

His first journey to West Virginia had started at Penn Station in Baltimore on Tuesday, June 9, 1964. His parents had dropped him off in time to catch the 3:00 p.m. train to Union Station in Washington, D.C. From there he had caught the westbound 6:00 p.m. train for the eight-hour train ride through the night through Maryland and West Virginia to the little town of Floydville, West Virginia, where his aunt would meet him and take him to the farm a short distance out of town.

It was still daylight during the first three to four hours of the journey and, except for the Washington metropolitan area he was leaving behind, there was nothing but trees, hills, rivers, and an occasional town along the way. The farther he travelled and the more rural the surroundings became, the more he began to wonder what his aunt and uncle had in store for him at the end of the long train ride.

Ron had only met them a couple of times when Uncle Fred was stationed at Fort Belvoir, Virginia, but he really didn't know them beyond what his mother had said about the "very odd pair." Aunt Jenny had been seven years older than his mother and had left home to go to college the year his mother entered the sixth grade. According to his mother, Aunt Jenny was a straight-laced, artsy, high school math teacher who should have been an old maid. Uncle Fred, in contrast, was a fun-loving and wise-cracking guy from West Virginia. The couple had met one night at the USO in Washington during World War II and had somehow managed to be happy together for reasons unbeknownst to the rest of the family.

It was when they moved to Uncle Fred's family farm in rural West Virginia after his retirement from the Army that Ron's mother had thought her sister had finally lost her mind.

As day became night, there was nothing but the constant sound of the wheels on the rails and total darkness outside except for the lights of an occasional railroad signal or small town they passed. The boy tried to sleep, but could not do so because of the loneliness, fear, and apprehension that had invaded him. He wanted to cry, but didn't want other passengers to see how alone and scared he was as the train carried him further to his exile from the life he knew and understood.

It was somewhat unnerving when the conductor announced, "Next stop is Floydville, West Virginia." It was shortly after 2:00 a.m. and all he could see were a few street and house lights as the train slowly made its way into town.

The depot was a small brick structure with nothing but a brick sidewalk and a steel-wheeled baggage cart outside. The lights were off and nobody was inside. In fact, there was nobody outside until Aunt Jenny appeared from around the corner of the building as he stepped off the train with his suitcase. He was relieved that she was on time because this looked like the worst place on earth to be stranded.

"Hi, Jamie," she said as she gave him a big hug. "How was the train ride?"

"Okay," replied the boy as he kept his tongue about being addressed by his childhood name, Jamie, which was short for his middle name and his late grandfather's first name.

"Are you hungry?" she asked. "I've got a couple of sandwiches for you in the car."

"No, I ate on the train," he replied, not wanting to admit that he had been too scared to leave his seat to do so.

He wished that she'd just be quiet and leave him alone. Surely she knew he didn't want to be here and didn't want to talk about it, especially in the middle of the night.

As they walked to the car, he suddenly realized that this place was quieter and cleaner than the city he had left a few hours before. It had rained earlier and the cool damp air was sweet and fresh instead of stagnant and full of the odors of vehicle exhaust, trash, and industrial pollution like the air he was used to smelling.

They drove through town and into the country. It wasn't much of a town and then there was nothing but darkness, silhouettes of wooded hillsides, and an occasional house along the road. A short time later, they turned onto a smaller macadam road and then onto a narrow gravel road that led to a little garage in the middle of nowhere.

"We're here," announced Aunt Jenny as she pulled into the garage and turned off the headlights and ignition of her shiny red Chevy.

He retrieved his suitcase from the trunk of the car and stepped outside. Before him was a large white Victorian house with a turret and ornate wooden trim like something one would see in a matinee ghost movie. The two trees in the yard with their twisted limbs made the scene even more unsettling.

Aunt Jenny ushered him through a little iron gate and through the yard to the big front porch where he waited while she opened the door and turned on the hall light. Once inside, she motioned for him to quietly follow her up the stairs to the second floor. After showing him where the bathroom was, she led him to a bedroom at the end of the hall, gave him a gentle kiss on the cheek, and said, "Good night." He went into the room, closed the door, and cried himself to sleep.

It was nearly noon when he finally woke up. After a quick bath, he dressed and made his way downstairs to the kitchen where Aunt Jenny was patiently waiting to prepare a late breakfast of eggs, fried potatoes, sausage, and fresh homemade biscuits. Aunt Jenny dispelled one concern that morning. They didn't plan to starve him to death.

Aunt Jenny next took him for a tour of the fifty-seven-acre farm in Uncle Fred's jeep. There was one cow, but no crops or other obvious signs of farming as Ron understood the term.

It was then that he made his first mistake of the summer when he said, "I certainly don't see a lot for me to do on this little one cow ranch."

Aunt Jenny gave him a stern look and replied in a direct, but gentle, manner, "There's plenty to keep you busy on this little one cow ranch like mowing the yard, tending the garden, caring for the cow and the chickens, and helping your Uncle Fred with whatever else he has for you. Am I clear?"

"Yes, as long as I don't have to do anything I don't want to do."

Aunt Jenny stared through him for a moment with her dark, piercing, eyes – a moment that seemed like hours – before saying as calmly as she had spoken to him before, "Jamie, my sister and your father love you very much and are afraid that you are heading in the wrong direction. That's why they asked us to take you in and help you get on the right track. We intend to hold up our end of the bargain and hope you are ready to hold up yours. If not, we'll put you back on the train and send you home to whatever fate awaits you there."

That was when the boy saw that Aunt Jenny was a master manipulator. She was one of those rare individuals who could get a person to do something she wanted done in a way that would make them ask how much they owed her for the privilege. He also saw that she was a straight talker and would, in a heartbeat, do what she said. She was not someone to mess with.

Uncle Fred arrived home shortly before 5:00 p.m. from his job as a supervisor for the gas company. Like most small-time farmers in the area, he had a regular job to support whatever farming he did.

He grabbed a cold beer from the refrigerator and invited the boy to join him on the porch while Aunt Jenny prepared dinner. Knowing that Uncle Fred had been a drill sergeant in the Army, Ron had expected him to start barking out orders and spelling out what he expected him to do for the rest of the summer. Instead, Uncle Fred sat there and chatted with him on a man to man basis. Best of all, he addressed him as Ron, young man, or soldier - depending upon the circumstances. Never did Uncle Fred call him Jamie, the name everybody except Aunt Jenny had stopped calling him when he was four or five. He thought she did it to get under his skin, so he accepted the name to show her that it didn't bother him.

After a little chitchat, Uncle Fred finally said, "Well, young man, I believe we're going to have some fun this summer."

"Doing what?"

"I've got some things I'd like for you to help me with while you're with us. I think we can get some of that baby fat off you as well."

The boy decided to let the second part of that go for now and asked, "What kind of things, sir?"

"First of all, don't call me sir," replied Uncle Fred. "I was a sergeant, not an officer. As for work, I could use your help keeping the equipment in shape, doing some maintenance work around the farm, and helping the men who are coming in to build an art studio for your aunt so she can paint to her heart's desire."

"I'd like to learn to drive the jeep, too, if that's all right."

"I think we can do that with no trouble."

"Don't forget about cleaning his room, mowing the yard, helping with the garden and chickens, and doing his math lessons," said Aunt Jenny, who had apparently been listening to their conversation.

"Of course," replied Uncle Fred. "We certainly wouldn't want to forget the administrative matters, would we?"

Ron decided right away that Uncle Fred was a pretty cool guy. This gave him hope that the summer here might not be as bad as he had thought it would be.

Uncle Fred took the young man upstairs after dinner, inventoried his belongings, and said, "Those are nice clothes you brought, but they won't stand up to the work on the farm. I'll ask your aunt to take you into town tomorrow and get you some boots, jeans, socks and shirts that will better serve you while you're with us."

"I didn't bring money for new clothes."

"We'll just call it standard issue. Now let's go outside and see how well you can handle a clutch."

Ron was driving the jeep in no time. As he drove around the farm and up and down the gravel road, Uncle Fred sat in the passenger seat explaining that his grandfather had settled this hollow and had divided it into three farms – one for each of his sons. One of his cousins, Clyde Warden, now owned the farm from the left side of the road to the ridge between his property and the mouth of the hollow and another cousin, James Smith with whom he was not on current speaking terms, owned the farm from the right side of road to the ridge between his property and the mouth of the hollow. Uncle Fred and Aunt Jenny's farm occupied the head of the hollow to the ridge. All of those details seemed unimportant to Ron at the time, but were important to Uncle Fred for some reason. What interested the boy most was the Warden girl, Joni, who smiled and waved as they passed her house. She was the most beautiful girl Ron had ever seen and he was suddenly in love.

As they arrived back at the farmhouse, Uncle Fred informed the boy that he was welcome to drive the jeep as long as he stayed within the limits of his farm, didn't harass or let the cow out, and didn't venture up the old gas well road to the ridge. He was also clear that he would suspend the boy's driving privileges immediately and permanently if he didn't comply.

Ron went to bed that night feeling like the summer here might not be as bad as he had thought. He was going to have to abide by the house rules and earn his keep, but he also had a vehicle to drive and the prettiest girl in the world next door. This place had possibilities and he was ready to stay and enjoy them to the fullest.

CHAPTER 3

Ron's second journey into the unknowns of West Virginia occurred exactly fifty-one years and three days after the first. The Monday morning flight from Houston to Pittsburgh was uneventful and on time. A short time later, he passed a WELCOME TO WILD WONDERFUL WEST VIRGINIA sign as he drove his rental car southward along Interstate 79. He took the Route 50 exit outside Clarksburg forty-five minutes later and found his way to his motel and a local Wal-Mart to get a detailed map book and a few supplies for his daily travels.

With all that completed, he returned to his room, readied his backpack, and went to the motel lounge for dinner and a drink. There was a Pittsburgh Pirates baseball game on the television that reminded him of long-ago summer evenings sitting on the porch with Uncle Fred listening to Pirates games on the radio. He returned to his room an hour or so later and turned in shortly thereafter. Tomorrow was going to be a long day.

Ron was up early Tuesday morning, had breakfast, and soon found himself heading westward on Route 50. It was a gloomy morning with light rain and fog on the surrounding hills. He remembered his uncle forecasting a day of rain by saying, "Fog on the hill means water at the mill." Hopefully it would not be a three-day front and he would have at least one sunny day to get out and explore. Whatever the impending weather might be, he was eager to see the old farm and hoped that whoever owned it now would let him look around.

It didn't take him long to see that there had been substantial changes in the area during the past fifty-one years. The most notable change was the presence of large open areas where busy factories had once stood. He suddenly asked himself, "What do people do for a living around here?"

Another notable change was the four-lane highway leading westward from Clarksburg. In 1964, Route 50 had been a twisting two-lane highway. Along the way he could see remnants of the old highway and a few familiar landmarks. He also recognized some little communities along the way, but not many.

The most surprising change was the absence of the railroad upon which he had arrived the last time he was here. Now there was a walking and biking trail where the railroad had once been.

He passed two exits for Floydville, the little

town where he had first arrived. A short time later, he saw the sign for the macadam road that led across the old railroad bed towards the farm. He turned onto the road and saw that, except for a few more houses along the way, nothing much had changed since the early 1960's. Ron Samuels felt like he was almost home.

A mile or so up the road was the familiar gravel road that led up the hollow to his destination. At the mouth of the hollow were the familiar Warden house on the left and the Smith house on the right. As he turned onto the gravel road, he could see the white Victorian farmhouse, now partially obscured by the fog, on the little knoll a quarter mile ahead. Beside the gate at the end of the driveway was a sign with the following words: EASY REST BED AND BREAKFAST, WELCOME. Ron eased the rental car up the hill and parked in the empty guest parking area. It was almost 8:40 a.m. and he hoped that somebody was there.

He opened the little gate that led into the yard and walked up the sidewalk to the house. It was obvious from what he could see through the fog that the house had been well cared for and that the yard and flower gardens were well tended. Aunt Jenny would have been proud of the place.

He rang the doorbell and waited with hope that he was not too early. A short time later, a lady with blondish gray hair answered the door.

He introduced himself and told her why I was there. She looked at him with a big smile on her face and said, "Jamie, it's you. Do you know who I am?"

His knees began to shake as he replied, "Yes, I bet you're Joni."

Her eyes filled with tears as she gave him a hug. "I didn't think I'd ever see you again.

How long are you staying?"

"I'm in the area until Friday."

"Where are you staying?"

"I've got a room at a motel on the other side of Clarksburg."

"Not anymore," she replied. "You can have your old room for ten percent less than those people are charging, including breakfast and dinner."

"I've already checked in for four nights and my belongings are still there."

"I have a doctor's appointment this morning not far from there. You can ride in with me, check out, and get your belongings before their checkout time. We can catch up on old times as we drive in."

"No," he replied, "I really don't want to bother you."

"I insist. Now step inside and have a seat while I get ready to go."

"I'll wait on the porch and call the motel to

say I'm checking out early. We can go in my rental car."

"Okay," she replied, "I'll be ready shortly."

He wondered if staying here was a good idea, but decided that it made a lot more sense than driving back and forth to Clarksburg. Staying on the farm in his old room might bring back some memories he hadn't expected. He also liked being called Jamie again. Why? He had no idea.

Ron was on his way back to Clarksburg ten minutes later with Joni as his tour guide. The day had already been full of pleasant surprises. Who would have guessed that he would be spending time with someone he had known that summer and would be sleeping tonight in his old bedroom? He was ready to stay.

CHAPTER 4

The first time he had ever spoken with Joni was his first Saturday in West Virginia. She and her mother were helping his aunt set up a picnic-style lunch for the men working in the hayfields. Aunt Jenny had called him over and introduced him to them. It had been an embarrassing encounter for him since Joni was a pretty sixteen-year-old girl with shorts, a white top, and silky-blond hair pulled back into a ponytail while he was a hot, sweaty, and half-dead fourteen-year-old boy in ugly work clothes and boots.

Joni had been polite, but had made it clear with her body language that she wasn't interested in him. It also didn't take long for her to drop the bomb that her seventeen-year-old boyfriend was going to pick her up shortly and take her to the lake for an afternoon of swimming with friends.

Joni had a younger brother, Jack, who was a couple of months older than Ron. Aunt Jenny had introduced the boys the day before while Jack was in the meadow on a tractor turning the cut grass in preparation for baling. The two boys became friends that summer, but Ron was jealous of Jack and tried – usually unsuccessfully – to compete with him tossing bales of hay, driving farm equipment, and most everything else.

Ron saw Joni many times that summer as he drove the jeep or tractor up and down the road, or when he visited her brother. She was usually on the porch reading a book, or in the yard sunbathing. She usually waved and said hello, but continued to have an air about her that told him that he was not going to be a member of her inner circle anytime soon. That didn't prevent him from drooling when he saw her, or from dreaming that someday she would come around. Yes, she was his first love, even if it was a totally one-sided affair.

The realization that he and Joni were never going to be a couple finally arrived on the Fourth of July. There had been hope early in the day when Joni and her brother had come up to fish with him in Uncle Fred's pond. That hope died in the afternoon when Joni lost all knowledge of her brother and him once her boyfriend and other friends arrived at the picnic at her parent's place. They were all together again that night watching the fireworks Uncle Fred and her father had purchased, but the camaraderie of the early morning was gone. She was still friendly, polite, and a casual friend thereafter, but showed no interest in him beyond that.

The last time Ron had seen her was during a

barbeque the evening before he returned to Baltimore. Joni, Jack, and Ron had a good time that evening socializing, eating, and pitching horseshoes together. She had then come up to him as he was leaving, gave him a sisterly hug, and asked him to send her a postcard. He never did.

CHAPTER 5

Ron could hardly believe that he was in the car with Joni, the girl he had never expected to see again. Before they had even gotten to the main road, Joni looked over at him and asked, "What have you been doing since you left?"

He didn't know how to respond since he had no idea what she had done or gone through during the same period of time. He had been successful, but didn't want to sound like a braggart. By the same token, he didn't want to be too unassuming since most people could see through that before it was even said.

After careful thought, he said, "I went back to Baltimore that fall and concentrated on improving my grades. I started playing football the following year and ended up going to the University of Maryland on an athletic scholarship."

"Don't tell me you went on to play professional football."

"No, I was a fourth string tackling dummy who quit after the first year to concentrate on mechanical engineering and Army ROTC. It seemed like a good idea after the low number I got in the military draft lottery in 1969."

"You must have gotten a good job and made a lot of money."

"I didn't get rich, but I've had steady work and a successful and interesting career."

"What did you do, anyway?"

"I spent four years in the Army, moved back to Baltimore, and spent the next twelve years as a maintenance and environmental engineer at a terminal facility. From there, I went to work for a big oil company in Houston and managed special environmental projects until they retired me early last week."

"That sounds pretty exciting."

"Not really. I was kind of like the man behind the elephant with a shovel."

"Did you travel much?"

"Yes, I did projects all over the United States, the Middle East, Asia, and South America."

"I always wanted to have a job where I could travel," replied Joni. "I thought about becoming an airline stewardess, but that dream didn't go very far."

"To be honest, Joni, travel gets old in a hurry. Most of my travels were to places you wouldn't want to go."

"Do you have family?"

"No, I lost my wife three years ago. We had no children."

"I'm sorry. I shouldn't have asked that question."

"That's okay. We had forty-two good years

together. I was blessed."

"Well," said Joni, "my life's been kind-of rough, too."

Ron found himself wishing that he had not gotten into this conversation. The only response he had for what she had just said was, "I hope it wasn't too rough."

"It started out well. I stayed at home and got a degree in elementary education from nearby Salem College. I wanted to get away from here after college and accepted a teaching position near Charleston. I really enjoyed working down there, living in a nice apartment with two other girls, and partying at night. Unfortunately, I met an irresponsible guy at a bar one night and fell in love with him. He seemed like a nice guy until we got married and I found that he was adverse to work and permanently stuck at age twenty-one. I tried to make it work, but gave up and divorced him after two years."

"Did you remarry?"

"Yes, but it took me four years to allow myself to fall in love and marry again. My second husband, Sam, was a kind, hard-working, and responsible man with a good job at one of the chemical plants outside Charleston. We had nineteen good years together before he died from a heart attack. He was only fifty."

"Did you have children?"

"Yes, we had one daughter who lives in Mom and Dad's home with her husband and two kids. You'll probably meet them before you leave."

"How did you end up in my aunt's old house?"

"That's an interesting story," replied Joni. "Your aunt and uncle started the bed and breakfast business in the late eighties. When he passed away in 1993, your aunt decided she couldn't maintain the farm and business by herself. She offered to sell Dad the whole farm, except the bed and breakfast. Dad made her an offer for the whole farm with the provision that she could stay in the house and run the bed and breakfast business as long as she wanted.

When she got sick and had to go to a nursing home in 2001, I sold my place in Charleston, moved back here, and bought her business. I inherited everything else when Dad and Mom died, so I guess I'm pretty well anchored here by a hundred and twenty acres, two old houses, and a bed and breakfast to keep me occupied."

"How long have your folks been gone?"

"Dad had a stroke and passed away in 2005. Mom passed away two years ago from congestive heart failure."

"What became of your brother?"

"Jack joined the Army as soon as he finished high school and was killed in a training accident in Germany in 1970."

"I'm sorry. I didn't know."

"That's all right. Now we've finally caught each other up on our old news."

Ron found himself with the perfect opportunity to change the subject and said, "It sounds like the bed and breakfast business has gone well."

"It has, except during the winter months. I only operate it from the first of April until the end of November unless someone has a special need."

"I'm surprised that I didn't see your business listed on the internet."

"I don't advertise on the internet. Most of my business comes from return clients or referrals. I also get a fair number of guests who come up here on weekends to ride their bikes on the rail trail that passes nearby."

"That's one of the first things I noticed driving here this morning. What happened to the railroad?"

"Passenger rail service through this area ended in the late 1960's and freight service ended sometime in the 1980's. The rails were removed and the railroad grade was turned into a seventy-two-mile-long hiking and biking trail extending all the way to Parkersburg. "

"Sounds like you have a busy place. Does your daughter help you with the business?"

"She helps some, but not much," replied Joni. "Both she and her husband have full-time jobs in Clarksburg. Her twelve-year-old daughter helps me with some of the inside work and her fourteen-year-old son helps with some of the outside work when I can get him moving."

"Does anybody farm the land?"

"Yes," she replied, "I lease it to a man who runs beef cattle on it. He keeps the fields mowed and the barns in shape as part of the agreement. I don't make a lot of money from the arrangement, but it helps me keep the place up and the taxes paid."

They arrived at the motel where Ron ran in, collected his belongings, and checked out with plenty of time to spare. He dropped her off at the doctor's office and drove around. It appeared that this particular area was thriving and that it had some of the same stores and chain restaurants he saw regularly in Houston.

Ron soon found himself back in the medical building parking lot waiting for Joni and hoping that whatever she was there for was nothing serious. She had sure had her share of bad luck and didn't need health issues at this stage of the game.

Joni came out of the building a few minutes later, got into the car, and said, "It looks like I'm good for another twelve thousand miles."

"Where do you want to go from here?" he asked.

"I'm ready for lunch and then have a couple of errands to run before we go home."

"Just point me in the right direction," he said with a laugh.

As we drove down the hill into Clarksburg, Ron noticed a familiar-looking area over the hill to the right. "What is that down there?"

"That's old Route 50. About all that's there now are car dealerships and a few old businesses. Why do you ask?"

"I don't know, but it looks familiar for some reason."

"Let's take the next exit and we can drive up there and see what you remember. There's also a nice Italian restaurant where we can have lunch."

They soon found themselves in the parking lot of the restaurant Aunt Jenny used to like. Being from Baltimore, she loved good Italian food and stopped there whenever she was in Clarksburg. Ron couldn't believe that the place was still here and that it hadn't changed much in the past fifty-plus years. The spaghetti and meatball dinner was also the best he had eaten in years.

It didn't take long for him to remember why old Route 50 looked so familiar. To the right was the car dealership where Aunt Jenny had brought her car for service. The little building up the road was where she had come to redeem trading stamps from purchases at various stores. The trading stamp business was now gone, but everything else looked much the same as he had remembered.

Ron then turned onto a little road to the left and soon remembered that it was the road that had led to the lumber company where he had come with Uncle Fred and one his friends to buy the lumber needed to convert the old cellar house into Aunt Jenny's art studio. As he looked out the window into the rain, he was again a fourteen-year-old boy sitting in an old farm truck enjoying the bumpy ride and listening to the funny stories the two men were telling. He could also envision the jug of clear liquid they occasionally drank from and the scolding they got from Aunt Jennie when they got home and watched as he unloaded most of the lumber. "The boy's gotta learn to work sometime," is all that Uncle Fred had said in reply.

"Are you okay?" Joni asked.

"Yes, I was just dreaming about the day I came up here to buy lumber with my uncle and one of his friends."

As they returned to the main road and made their way into Clarksburg, Ron couldn't help but wonder how little events in the life of a man who had travelled the world could be remembered and appreciated after so many years. He had no answer, but was glad that they had made that little side trip into his past.

The one-way street through town looked both familiar and foreign. It was obvious that time had not been good to this community.

Stores he had remembered were gone and there didn't seem to be much happening. After a stop at the grocery store, they drove back to the farm. It was still raining and everything looked gloomy. Joni began to point out various landmarks along the way and to tell him a little about each. As they passed through an area where there had once been substantially more activity than there was now, Ron finally said, "I've noticed that this little part of the world doesn't seem to be very prosperous anymore. What happened?"

Joni looked at him with a sad expression on her face and replied, "Around the time I moved to Charleston, there was a big push for four-lane highways, malls, and consolidation of schools, medical facilities and other services. People called it progress and hoped that it was the beginning of an influx of people, businesses, and high paying jobs. Instead, it ended up isolating and hurting a lot of small communities since commerce, schools, and services moved over time into the consolidated developments near hubs along the major highways."

"What happened to the factories and businesses that were already here?"

"That was the other part of the problem. As things were consolidating, factories were beginning to close or move out, the mining industry was slowing, and a lot of small business owners were retiring. Except for some government jobs that came in a few years ago, nothing much has come in to replace what has been lost."

"What do people do now?"

"Some people work for oil and gas, utility, or mining and industrial businesses that still remain. Others work for the government and available commercial and service jobs. Everybody else is retired, disabled, or looking for work. It's not as bad here as in some parts of the state, but there's still a problem."

"Maybe things will start improving now that the economy seems to be recovering. With the good roads, natural resources, available workforce, and comfortable lifestyle, I would think this area could be a magnet for high tech or tourist-related businesses. Fran and I used to get out of Houston occasionally and travel to areas that had become tourist traps with antique shops, old-time stores, boutique restaurants, and the like. Why couldn't it happen here?"

"A developer is currently planning to convert the old factory complex in Floydville into some kind of theme park with shops, restaurants, entertainment, and the like. There is a lot of hope that it will spur tourist-related jobs, but many of us around here wonder if there will be enough interest, political push, money, or local non-seasonal business to make it sustainable. We've been disappointed before."

Ron could see from their conversation today that Joni was no longer the Joni Warden he had known half a century ago. She was a woman who had been through adversity and who had the fighting spirit to pick her up time after time and thrive with what she had to work with. He could also see that she had a darned good understanding of the dynamics of the surrounding area and business in general. He could also see hope, yet skepticism that conditions around here were going to get better anytime soon.

CHAPTER 6

It was still raining when they arrived at the farm, but the fog had lifted. The entire farmhouse was now visible and Ron could see the familiar turret, silver metal roof, ornate woodwork, and wrap-around front porch with the fancy wooden columns. Nothing seemed to have changed over the years, including the two porch swings and large wicker chairs on the front porch.

They unloaded the car and carried the supplies Joni had purchased to the picnic table on the covered patio at the back of the house. The ends of the patio had been enclosed and the far end had been further enclosed and converted into a sun room with a red tile floor, lots of small windows, and leisure furniture. The style of the sun room and furnishings suggested that the improvements had probably been one of Aunt Jenny's long-ago projects.

Directly across the patio from the kitchen door was the stone cellar where Aunt Jenny had kept her canned goods and anything else she wanted to keep cool. Beside the cellar were concrete stairs that led up to the cellar house that had been transformed into the art studio.

Joni told him to get his belongings and she would give him a tour of the house as she showed him to his room. As he entered kitchen door, he found himself inside the farmhouse for the first time in over fifty years. Except for some fresh paint on the walls, new appliances, and different curtains, the kitchen looked the same as it had looked the day he left in August, 1964. Ron mentioned this to Joni and she revealed that she had loved the kitchen as it was and had chosen not to remodel it beyond replacing the sink, plumbing fixtures, and linoleum with materials closely resembling the originals. Even the modern appliances were of a style that resembled the originals.

They passed through the dining room and parlor to the front of the house. The darkened rooms with high ceilings, ornate woodwork, flowery wallpaper, hardwood floors partially covered with Persian-style carpets, dark burgundy curtains with white pull-down shades, and dark wooden pocket doors between the rooms were also as Ron had remembered. He laughed and told Joni how unfriendly and spooky these rooms had appeared the morning he first walked through them and how he had expected something or someone to jump out and grab him as he walked through.

In the corner of the parlor sat a familiar piece of furniture. "That looks like the desk where Aunt Jenny force-fed algebra to me that summer."

"It probably is," replied Joni. "Everything here is original except for the new wallpaper and window dressings, fresh varnish, and your aunt's paintings on the walls. Why change perfection?"

"Aunt Jenny would certainly be pleased."

"I'd be afraid she would come back and haunt me if she wasn't."

It was not until they had gone upstairs and Ron entered his old bedroom that the full effect of the old house hit him. Like everything else he had seen, this room had changed little since he had walked out and closed the door that long-ago August morning. The big metal-frame bed, wooden dresser, table, and closet in the corner looked the same. The two screened and wavy hand-made window glass windows, long white curtains, and pull-down shades were exactly as he had remembered. The only things he didn't recognize were the new and more subdued wallpaper and the painting above the dresser. It was that of a boy in bib overalls, a white T-shirt, brown work boots, and red baseball hat sitting in the seat of an old Ford tractor. Tears formed in his eyes when he recognized that it was a portrait of him.

Joni looked at him and said, "Your aunt always called this 'Jamie's Room.' It's been a favorite of our guests."

Ron now understood why Joni had called him Jamie all morning.

"Why don't you make yourself comfortable and rest awhile? You can see the remainder of the house later."

Joni left the room and closed the door. Ron sat on the bed and composed himself before he walked to the side window, raised the shade, and looked out. The rain had stopped and the fog had nearly disappeared from the rest of the valley. Through the wavy glass he could see the old barn, the meadow with grazing black beef cows, the small creek now flowing full and muddy, and the wooded hillside beyond.

He went to the back window and looked out. There was the cellar house, garden, and wooded hillside that extended from the back of the house to the ridge. Below the window was the patio roof that was, as Uncle Fred had informed him at least once a week, his first avenue of escape in the event of a fire.

He opened both windows a few inches to get a cross breeze flowing through the room. The house still didn't have air conditioning, or at least none in he could detect.

With that completed, he changed into a T-shirt and shorts and climbed into bed for a short nap. He just lay there between the fresh sheets enjoying the fresh country air flowing through the room and the sweet smells of the old house and farm outside. Before he knew it, he was sound asleep in his old bed.

When he awakened, he'd been asleep for

two and a half hours and it was now late afternoon. He arrived downstairs shortly thereafter and found Joni in the kitchen making sandwiches. She said that she had gotten a call from the local funeral director and was awaiting the arrival of two couples who would be staying in the other upstairs bedrooms for two nights while they were in town for a funeral. She said that she was preparing a sandwich tray for them and asked if he would like to have a chicken salad sandwich and some iced tea. He readily accepted.

Ron then asked if he could see the cellar house where he had spent a substantial amount of time that summer. She said that it was the next place she had planned to take him.

As they entered the room, Ron recognized the windows, knotty pine tongue and groove walls, white tile ceiling with inset lights, and varnished pine floor he had helped install. The room brought back fond memories of the hard work he had put in and the teasing he had gotten from the two teachers Uncle Fred had hired to do the work. Most of all, he remembered the pride and satisfaction he had experienced seeing the fruit of his labor, although he had mainly carried and held things for those doing the actual work. It was a joy to be here and see it again.

Joni told him of her dream of someday converting the studio into a bunk room and the downstairs sun room into a common area for young hikers and bikers who needed a place to stay, but couldn't afford the full bed and breakfast rates. "Dreams take money," she finally said, "so I don't think it'll ever be a reality."

Ron decided to take one last trip, this one alone, to the basement before retiring to the front porch. He didn't know why he wanted to go down there, but he did. The place consisted of two dark, dreary, and mostly empty rooms. The main room contained some old furniture and what appeared to be a relatively new gas furnace. The old furnace, or maybe the associated duct work, occasionally made a terrible rumbling sound. He had nearly jumped out of his skin when he first heard it.

The second and smaller room still smelled like sulfur from the days when it was used to store coal before the original furnace was converted to natural gas. Along the outer wall was a metal door and chute which had once been used to place coal in the room. It was through this little door that he had helped deliver boxes of liquor his uncle stored in a locked cabinet in the corner – the Class Six locker as Uncle Fred called it – for sale by the drink to a small and trusted clientele. The cabinet was still there with the affixed military-style padlock. Ron started laughing and decided to see if there was any liquor in the cabinet after all these years. A careful survey of one of the overhead floor joists revealed a little hook with the spare key for the lock. He emerged from the basement a short time later with an unopened bottle of bourbon. He planned to open it and have a high ball in memory of Uncle Fred if the liquor was still good. Surely it hadn't gone bad in an unopened bottle kept in a cool dry place like the Class Six locker.

With his cold drink in hand, Ron retired to one of the wicker chairs on front porch. It didn't take long for him to remember how cool the evening breeze could be in the late spring, especially after a day of rain. After a quick trip upstairs, he was back on the porch with a jacket, and hat.

Night began to set in and everything became dark except for the stars, moon, and distant lights from the houses down the hollow. The only sounds were those of cicadas, tree frogs, and an occasional car on the distant road. He thought for a moment that he saw Aunt Jenny and Uncle Fred sitting in the porch swing together with Uncle Fred playfully poking her in the ribs and Aunt Jenny smilingly telling him to behave with guests around.

He didn't know if it was his memories of those nights on the porch or the bourbon which he rarely partook of, but he suddenly realized that this place was where he had been really loved and wanted for the first time. His parents had been good people and had certainly loved him, but his father was always too busy to spend time with him and his mother was either working, or busy trying to impress her little social group. With his aunt and uncle here on the farm, he had felt like he was in a normal family who put their work aside in the evening, sat down together for dinner, and relaxed on the porch with each other in the cool evening air.

His reflections of the past were interrupted when two cars with Joni's guests came up the driveway. She ushered them through the front door, turned, and said, "It's getting cold out here. Maybe you'd be more comfortable in the sun room."

"No," he replied, "I'd like to sit here awhile and enjoy the porch again."

The next thing he knew, he was waking up in the middle of the night and slowly making his way up the stairs to his room like he had done so many times that summer. It was a wonderful feeling.

CHAPTER 7

Ron was awakened by the sun shining through the side window and the smell of something sweet in the kitchen below. He quickly showered, changed into casual clothes, and made his way to the kitchen where Joni was taking fresh-made scones from the oven. On the counter were a pot of hot coffee, bran muffins, and freshly-made granola she had just finished making for her guests.

Joni looked up, smiled, and said, "Good morning, sleepy head. Do you want a continental breakfast, or an old fashioned country breakfast?"

"I'll have coffee and a couple of scones," he replied. "Everything looks and smells so good."

He finished breakfast and helped her carry everything into the dining room for her other guests. "What are you going to do today?" she asked.

"I think I'll take a tour of the farm. Do you still have the old jeep?"

"It's in the back of the barn, but I doubt if it'll run. You can take my four-wheeler instead. It's in the garage."

Ron left the house and found what she called a four-wheeler. It was a hardtop all terrain vehicle with seats for two, a windshield with wipers, cloth side curtains, and a cargo bed. To the side was a snow blade that could be installed for winter service. She was certainly prepared for whatever might come to pass.

He drove down the driveway and entered the gate that led into the pasture where several beef cattle were grazing. Seeing the cattle reminded him of the story Aunt Jenny had told him about the lone cow that had once roamed the range. It started one rainy Sunday afternoon when Uncle Fred and one of his drinking buddies decided to buy a calf, raise it, and butcher it in the fall for meat. She said she had not believed that they were serious until Uncle Fred showed up a couple of nights later with the materials needed to fence in the lower end of the meadow. Two weeks later, the two men were in the cattle business.

His first stop was the barn. It looked much the same as it had in 1964, except for a new metal roof, fresh paint, and the absence of the chicken coop that had once been attached to the side towards the house. How he had hated those chickens. Even killing and preparing them for dinner was a messy and smelly affair.

He opened the big barn doors and found himself in the place where he had shoveled cow manure, lubed and maintained the farm equipment, and made enough noise to convince Aunt Jenny that he was always gainfully employed. In the back corner was the jeep, now covered with layers of boxes, assorted junk, and about an inch of dust. It would take a major effort to uncover it, let alone get it running again. In the center of the barn was the old Ford tractor that appeared to have been well maintained and in a serviceable condition. Ron hopped into the seat, re-familiarized himself with the gears and controls, and turned the key. It started. He drove it outside, exercised the cutting bar on weeds around the barn, and returned it to the barn. That felt good.

He then climbed the wooden ladder to the hayloft. This is where he had worked so hard stacking hay bales during his first Saturday in West Virginia and where he had later spent many hours shooting groundhogs with the .22 rifle that Uncle Fred had taught him to shoot.

That had been his most enjoyable and profitable chore that summer with the one dollar per groundhog bounty Uncle Fred had paid him for eradicating the varmints, burying them, and filling the holes they had made in the meadow. The training and practice with that little rifle had also served him well in the Army.

He closed the barn doors, climbed back into the four-wheeler and explored the remainder of the farm over the same general route he and Uncle Fred had taken during his first day here. Nothing much had changed except for the relocation of some of the fences and a larger number of cattle in the fields. It appeared to him that the farmer had better mow the meadow and get the first cutting of hay in the barn. He thought about taking the four-wheeler up the old well road to the ridge, but decided he'd better get Joni's permission before doing so.

The next stop was the two-acre pond in the side hollow behind the barn. The pond was much the same as he had remembered, but the area around it had not been mowed and maintained as Uncle Fred had liked it.

It was at the pond, or more specifically in the wetland area above it, that he had learned the drill sergeant side of Uncle Fred. It happened the Monday of his second week there. The whole affair started when he complained about Aunt Jenny's itinerary for the day that included cleaning the barn, mowing and trimming the lawn, and accompanying her to town. He was still tired and sore from working in the hayfield two days before and wanted to do nothing but relax, recover, and drive the jeep around the farm. Aunt Jenny had other ideas.

It was late afternoon when they arrived home and Aunt Jenny gave him permission to drive the jeep as long as he stayed in meadow or on the gravel road where she could see or hear him. He soon found himself up the side hollow trying to drive around the pond by way of a wetland. The next thing he knew, the jeep was up to the axles in mud and muck. The more he tried to get out, the deeper the jeep sank.

Uncle Fred was home by the time he arrived at the house on-foot, tired, sweaty, and covered from head to foot with mud. After dinner, which he ate at the outside picnic table, Uncle Fred took him back to the pond on the tractor. The man's face turned bright red and his knuckles tightened on the steering wheel when he saw his prized possession floating in the wet goo. He didn't scream, but instead gave the boy a dose of his biting wit and sarcasm by saying, "That's beautiful, soldier. In twenty-two years in this man's Army, including two bloody wars, I've never witnessed such a masterful job of burying a jeep."

The message had been clear and stung like a bee. Next came the instructional phase of the young man's ordeal when Uncle Fred added, "It's now time for a little vehicle recovery and maintenance training."

Ron's training started with a trip into the muddy mess to attach a chain to the partially-buried towing ring on the back of the jeep. He was then instructed to climb into the slippery interior of the jeep, take it out of gear, and steer as Uncle Fred pulled it out of the muck with the tractor. The training continued a short time later in the shallow part of the creek near the barn where Uncle Fred instructed him to drive the vehicle up and down the creek bed to remove as much mud and muck as possible before washing it with rags and lubing it at all the places he pointed out.

Ron was back at the house an hour or so later where Uncle Fred inspected the cleaned and fully lubed jeep and declared that an outstanding job had been done. He then instructed the boy to go to the back of the house, strip to his skin, and leave his wet and dirty clothes and boots on the back porch before proceeding through the house to the shower while Uncle Fred diverted Aunt Jenny's attention in the front yard.

As he quietly came to the front door after his shower and change into clean clothes, Ron heard Uncle Fred and Aunt Jenny talking on the porch. She was saying in a low, but stern voice, "You don't have to kill him. He's still a boy."

"I won't kill him. He reminds me too much of me."

The remainder of the evening was spent quietly on the porch together. Uncle Fred excused himself to go back into the house to refill his drink and to bring the boy something cold to drink. Ron's eyes must have nearly jumped out of his head when he took his first sip because Aunt Jenny looked at Uncle Fred and said, "Fred, he's too young for that foolishness."

"There's not enough in it to hurt him. Anyway, he earned it." The drink apparently didn't hurt him, but it along with the evening's festivities had put him into a deep sleep. Ron woke up in the chair sometime during the night. On the little table beside him were his washed, dried, and neatly-folded clothes, underwear and all. Ron never knew who washed them, but suspected that it had been his uncle.

As Ron sat by the pond thinking, he realized that the events of that long-ago evening had probably been the turning point in his life. Not only had Uncle Fred broken his boyhood stubbornness and pride; he had shown the boy that he really cared and was willing do whatever it took to teach him to be a man, provided that he was willing to learn.

The learning process continued the following evening when Uncle Fred came home from work with a fishing rod, reel, and small metal tackle box for him. Ron never knew if it had been a peace offering, or if his uncle had just wanted a fishing buddy. Whatever the reason, it served both purposes.

As he looked at the little peninsula that extended into the pond, Ron envisioned the two of them sitting on camp stools and talking as they fished together into the night. The pond became their special hiding place where they would listen to Pirate baseball games on the radio, discuss the happenings of the day, and have a cold beer together without Aunt Jenny around to complain. "Fishing sure makes a man thirsty," is what Uncle Fred would always say as he handed over the "church key" used to open beer cans back then. Most importantly, Uncle Fred shared many stories and little bits of wisdom with him, something that his father never did.

Ron felt the urge to go fishing again and was soon in the barn looking for his old fishing tackle. Under the work bench was the little metal tackle where he had left it. Everything appeared to be in order except for the deteriorated rubber worms in the till. His old fishing rod was hanging across two nails in a wooden joist over the bench. All that appeared to be needed was a good cleaning, some oil on the reel, and new fishing line.

It also occurred to him that the grass around the pond needed to be cut before he could safely walk around and fish. Would Joni give him permission to use the old tractor to mow the area so he could fish? All he could do was to ask.

Joni laughed when he returned to the house and told her his plans. "It's fine with me if you promise not to kill yourself."

"Kill myself on that old tractor?" he asked

with a grin. "There's a painting upstairs showing I know what I'm doing. I'll get some gas for it while I'm in town getting some fishing line and oil for my old reel."

"Could you pick up a few items for me at the feed and hardware store? I'll call Dickey Spence and tell him what I need."

Fifteen minutes later, Ron was on his way to Floydville with an empty five-gallon gasoline can.

CHAPTER 8

Floydville was still a nice place, but Ron could see that it wasn't the thriving little town it had once been. There was hardly any traffic since most everybody bypassed the town now. There were still many nice homes, but there were also more than a few that were abandoned and badly deteriorated from lack of normal maintenance. The small downtown area also had fewer businesses than he had remembered. About all that was there now were small grocery store, pharmacy, restaurant, tavern, and a few other small establishments. Missing were the theater and the clothing store where Aunt Jenny had bought his work clothing the day after he had arrived.

In the middle of town was the feed and hardware store where he and Uncle Fred had stopped many times. The owner, Dickey Spence, met him as he walked in the door.

"You must be Ron Samuels. Joni Marcum called and told me you were on your way."

"Yes, and you must be Mr. Spence."

"Call me Dickey. Mr. Spence was my dad. Joni said you're the nephew who lived with the Strivers one summer years ago. What brings you back to Floydville?"

"I just retired and decided to take a trip back here to look around and see if there is anything or anybody I could remember from my summer here in 1964."

"I don't know if you remember me, but I'm the kid who used to hang around here with my father and grandfather. I'm the third generation owner."

"Dickey, I'd like to stay and talk, but I really

have to take care of some other business and get back to the farm. I'd like to pick up the items Joni ordered and buy some fishing line, reel oil, and a couple of rubber worms if you have them."

Ron left the feed and hardware store a short time later with the items he'd come for, plus some hooks and sinkers required to rig the plastic worms the way fishermen do now. Apparently they quit making the pre-rigged worms he had been familiar with years ago.

His next stop was the local diner for a quick burger before returning to the farm. He wondered if he would run into anybody else who remembered him and, more importantly, how soon rumors might start about him staying at Joni's place.

Lunch went well with no more encounters except for an occasional glance from someone wondering who the stranger might be. The only inquiry was from the lady at the cash register who said, "You must be new in town."

"I'm just here visiting for a couple of days," is all that he volunteered.

Dickey Spence and the local policeman entered the diner as he turned to leave. "Have a good day, Mr. Samuels. This is Dan McGrew, our police chief. His dad was chief back when you were here."

"Nice to meet you, Mr. McGrew," he replied, now hoping to get out of the place before the friendly proprietor of the feed and hardware store and his friend could engage him in further conversation.

The last stop was the gasoline station near the highway exit at the western end of the town to fill the five-gallon gas can. He was on the tractor mowing the grass along the edge of the pond less than an hour later.

The work took most of the afternoon. Ron could have stopped sooner, but couldn't bring himself to quit until the entire meadow around the pond had been mowed. He put the tractor away, serviced it the way Uncle Fred had instructed, and went to the house hot, dirty, sunburned, and satisfied with what he had just accomplished. The fourteen-year-old boy in him was quickly reverting back to the sixty-five-year-old man who wondered how he would feel in the morning.

Ron retreated to the back porch after dinner to disassemble, clean, oil, and re-line his old fishing reel. It was not long before he was on the front lawn practicing his casting. Joni watched from the front porch and sarcastically asked, "Are you catching anything out there?"

"No, but I hope to catch some fish for breakfast in the morning."

"I can't cook them tomorrow morning, but could make you an old fashioned fish breakfast before you leave Friday."

"I wouldn't want to put you out, Joni. That's a lot of work."

"I've been looking for an excuse to have fish for breakfast. If you catch 'em, I'll cook 'em. Is that a deal?"

"It's a deal."

Ron was in bed early that night. It was going to be an early morning and he was too tired, stiff, and sore from the day's work to sit on the porch in the cool evening air.

CHAPTER 9

The alarm rang at 4:30 a.m. Ron dressed and slipped quietly into the kitchen to load his backpack with the sandwich, muffin, and two bottles of water Joni had left in the refrigerator for him. A short time later, he was heading to the pond in the four-wheeler with the fishing gear he had loaded the night before. The only thing he hadn't done was dig fishing worms, so he would be fishing with the plastic worms he had purchased the day before. He just hoped that he could remember how Dickey Spence had shown him to rig them.

It was still too dark to see what he was doing when he arrived at the pond, so he sat in the vehicle, ate the sandwich and muffin, and enjoyed the peacefulness of the place. He rigged his fishing rod and started fishing as the sun began to rise above the adjacent ridge and the pond became visible through the early morning mist.

The first cast of the day was into the deep hole at the base of a willow tree that hung over the edge of the pond. The rod nearly jumped from his hand when the fish took the worm as it sank to the bottom. Ron pulled a 20-inch largemouth bass from the water a few minutes later, admired it, and released it. Uncle Fred had always insisted that the large bass should be returned to the water to maintain a healthy gene pool in the pond.

He slowly walked around the pond casting into areas likely to hold nice bass. He caught several more fish, all smaller than the first. Of these, he put two ten-inch bass on the stringer for tomorrow's breakfast. That was a delicacy Uncle Fred had prepared for breakfast on weekends and one Ron looked forward to having again.

Ron returned from his little expedition and found Joni in the kitchen preparing breakfast for her guests. Helping her was her twelve-year-old granddaughter, Mary. The girl was a younger version of her grandmother as Ron had known her over fifty years ago. She was neatly dressed and had her grandmother's charm and friendliness.

Mary's fourteen-year-old brother, Jeffrey, was sitting at the kitchen table playing a video game. He was sloppily dressed and more interested in the video game than his grandmother, sister, or their guest. Ron realized that he was looking at his fourteen-year-old self and didn't like what he saw. This kid needed a good dose of Aunt Jennie and Uncle Fred.

"Are you ready for breakfast?" asked Joni.

"Sure, but I'd better clean the fish and

shower first."

Ron was back in the kitchen forty-five minutes later, all cleaned up and dressed. As they were eating breakfast together, he asked, "Is there anything I can do for you before I visit the cemetery?"

"I'm fine," replied Joni. "Mary's going to help me get things ready for the funeral dinner and Jeffrey's going to mow and trim the yard."

Jeffrey looked up from his video game and replied, "I already have plans this morning. The yard looks fine the way it is."

"No, it's not fine. Get out there and do what I asked."

"Grandma, it's too wet to mow now. I'll do it when I get back from my ride up the hollow in the four-wheeler."

Ron wanted to say something, but held his tongue. It was good that he did since Joni looked sternly at the young man and said, "You can sit there all day if you like, but the four-wheeler is going to stay in the garage until all the work around here is completed. Do you comprehend what I'm saying?"

"Okay, I'll do it."

That did it. Taking the wheels from a boy still works.

Ron's itinerary for the day included a visit to the graves of Aunt Jenny and Uncle Fred, the part of this trip he was looking forward to the least. He hated cemeteries, especially those where his wife and other close relatives were buried.

He stopped in Floydville to pick up the flower arrangements Joni had ordered for him at the florist. With the flower arrangements in the trunk, he followed her directions to a narrow country road that led out of town to the cemetery. He turned at the sign for the cemetery and carefully followed a winding gravel trail that traversed up a steep hill, through an open iron gate, and around the ridge to the place where Joni said the graves were located.

On the hillside about ten yards from the road was a tombstone with STRIVER engraved on it. In front of the tombstone were two metal pots with flower arrangements from the recent Memorial Day. Each had the same kinds of flowers as the fresh arrangements he had brought. Joni must have placed them there when she decorated the graves of her family members who were also buried nearby.

Ron replaced the flower arrangements, knelt, and read the engraved names and dates on the tombstone - the only physical reminder that these two people had once lived. Tears flowed as he thanked them for all that they had done for him and apologized for not keeping in touch with them while they were still living. He knew that they couldn't hear him, but it felt comforting to ask for their forgiveness anyway. After a short prayer, he got up and walked back to the car with the old flowers. It was the first time during his trip that Ron felt truly at peace with himself.

It was a little before noon when he arrived in town, but he wasn't hungry or interested in going into the diner and being the main attraction for the local lunchtime crowd. Instead, he parked in the small lot beside the former train depot and started walking eastward along the hiking and biking trail that had once been a railroad. Half a mile or so down the trail he found the old factory that was going to be converted into some sort of tourist attraction. Something was definitely happening since there was an abundance of heavy equipment and manpower removing machinery, demolishing some buildings, and power washing others. Maybe something like this would to spur the local economy. He sure hoped it would for the sake of people like Joni.

A short time later, he was back at the depot

sitting at a trailside picnic table and having a sandwich and soda from a nearby convenience store. A man whom he had seen at the convenience store walked over to the picnic table and asked, "Are you Fred Striver's nephew?"

"Yes, Ron Samuels is the name. Who do I have the pleasure of speaking with?"

"You may not want to know," replied the man with a grin on his face. "I'm Charlie England, the guy whose nose you broke the last time you were in town."

It had happened in late July while he, Aunt Jenny, and Uncle Fred were in town for the annual carnival. A cute little brunette came up to him and asked if he would take her on the Ferris wheel. She said her boyfriend, who happened to be the town bully, Charlie England, was afraid to ride it with her. Ron readily agreed and found himself face to face with Charlie and three of his friends as he and the girl disembarked.

"What are you doing with my girlfriend?" England had asked.

"I just took her for a ride on this thing. She said you were afraid to ride it with her."

That had apparently been the wrong thing to say since young Mr. England said, "that's a lie, city boy," as he drew a fist and threw a sucker punch at Ron.

Ron had anticipated the punch, moved his head to the side, and came up with a short and nearly invisible jab that flattened the bully's nose. That had been the end of the fight, but not the end of the affair. Uncle Fred paraded him through the crowd like a triumphant Roman general which both embarrassed and angered Aunt Jenny, who quietly slipped across the railing behind the bingo stand, met them at the car, and reprimanded them all the way home. It was also the last time she took him, or allowed him to be taken, into

Floydville until the day he caught the train home. Ron never knew if it was because Aunt Jenny had been too embarrassed to be seen in town with him, or if she had taken seriously rumors that Charlie and his friends intended to exact revenge if they saw him in town again. Now Charlie England and he were finally face to face again.

Charlie held out his hand and said, "I just wanted to stop and tell you what I thought of your uncle. If it hadn't been for him, I'd probably be dead, in prison, or both by now."

"Really?" asked Ron with relief that the subject of revenge for the broken nose had not come up. "That's two of us."

"I was a mess when I returned from Vietnam. All I wanted to do was drink, fight, and smoke grass. Your uncle was in Sarge's Place, a bar here in town back then, and told me to start acting like a soldier and a man before I screwed up and got myself into trouble I couldn't get out of. I told him to keep his advice to himself, or that I'd kick his butt. You know what he did?"

"No, but I can guess."

"He looked me straight in the eye, smiled, and said, 'Young man, you're not the first man who's tried. If you need help, call me and I'll do anything I can do for you. If you want to screw up your life, it's not my place to stop you.' He then put his nearly-full mug down, dropped some money on the bar, and walked out on me."

"What happened then?"

"I called him one night and asked for help. He picked me up and took me to his place for a talk. Things began to change that night and he got me back on track. He later stood up for me and got me a job with the gas company. I retired with forty-two years of service before they gave me the golden boot. I asked him one time why he helped a jerk like me and how I could ever repay him for it. He just said, 'Charlie, you reminded me of myself when I came back from the Pacific. Someone helped me and I just passed it on. You do the same for someone else. That's all I ask you to do in return.' Anyway, I thought you'd like to know."

"Thanks, Charlie," replied Ron. "That explains a lot. By the way, I'd like to apologize about the nose."

"I wasn't going to mention it, but Fred never let me live it down. In fact, he was proud of you for a lot of things and never stopped talking about you, or your travels and accomplishments."

"By the way, what became of the girl? I think her name was Doris."

"You spoke to her yesterday at the diner. She owns the place and also happens to be my wife for over forty-seven years."

"Is she worried about the new restaurants

coming into town? I saw them working at the old factory site."

"I'm hoping she'll retire and sell the diner so we can get out of here and travel while we can. It was her parents' place, so she doesn't want to see it close. The kids live out of state and don't want it. I don't know anyone here who would want it either."

"My wife and I were going to retire and travel, but she got sick and died before it could happen."

"Sorry, I didn't know."

"That's okay. We had a good life together."

"Did you have any kids?"

"No, we were always too busy to have kids. I guess that's why I'm having such a difficult time figuring out what I'm going to do with myself now that I've finally retired."

"So you just retired?"

"Yes," replied Ron, "I got what you called the golden boot last week. I came back here trying to find my bearings so I can decide what to do next. There's nothing left for me in Houston and certainly nothing back in Baltimore where my wife and I were both from."

"Why don't you move back here?"

"What would a workaholic engineer do around here?"

"Well," replied Charlie with a grin, "I know where you might find a small town diner to run."

The two men shared a hardy laugh before Charlie said, "Dickey told me that you're a fisherman. Why don't you go with me to my mountain camp this weekend? There should be a few trout left in the stream."

It was then that Ron began to wonder what was going around town about him and what he should and shouldn't say. "If you call a guy who goes fishing in a farm pond once in over fifty years a fisherman, then I guess I'm guilty.

Thanks for the invitation, but I'm going back to Houston tomorrow morning."

"Why don't you plan on coming back in mid-October? That's when they stock some of the streams with a few big trout. If nothing else, it's a good time to get out, enjoy the cool fall air, and see the mountains in full fall color."

"Maybe I'll take you up on that. Let me put your email address and phone number in my phone so I can get in touch with you."

Once they had shared contact information, Ron looked at his watch and said, "It's been great seeing you again, Charlie, but I really need to be getting back to the EASY REST."

"So that's where you're staying," replied Charlie as if he didn't know it already. "Joni has a nice place out there. I don't know how she keeps it going by herself. Her daughter and son-in-law sure don't help her much from what my wife tells me."

"She definitely keeps the place up nice," replied Ron. "My aunt and uncle would be proud of her."

"Just between the two of us, Ron, you wouldn't go wrong if you got yourself hooked up with Joni. There'd be plenty out there to keep you occupied and she's one of the nicest and most respected people around here. Still pretty good looking, too, if you ask me."

"Thanks, Charlie, but I'm not ready for anything like that," replied Ron as he politely extricated himself from the conversation before something would be said or implied that would become fodder for small town gossip. Neither he, nor Joni, needed that.

CHAPTER 10

Ron stopped at the florist to pick up a flower arrangement for Joni. It was the least he could do to repay her for the hospitality and help with ordering the flowers for the cemetery. He hoped that the lady at the florist shop hadn't gotten the wrong idea, so he clearly explained that it was a little thank you present.

He arrived at the farm and saw that all the guest traffic had left. Hearing or seeing nobody as he quietly slipped through the front door, he moved the artificial flower arrangement off the mantle in the parlor and replaced it with the fresh flowers. He then hid the old arrangement behind the sofa before asking in a rather loud voice, "Is anyone home?"

"Nobody but us mice," replied Joni from the

kitchen. "I'm finishing up and getting ready to rest for awhile. You don't mind if we have a late dinner, do you?"

"That sounds good to me. I think I'll go up to my room and take a nap. What time should I come down?"

"Come on down whenever you wake up. It's a nice day, so I thought we'd have a little picnic."

When he got to his room, Ron found that his soiled clothes had been washed, folded, and neatly placed on his bed. When had that woman found the time to do that?

Bathed, rested, and in fresh clothes, he walked into the kitchen as Joni closed the lid on an ice chest. She looked up and said, "You can carry this out to the four-wheeler. We're going to have our picnic in my gazebo on the ridge. I sent Jeffrey up there with a broom and mop earlier today and hope he cleaned everything like he was supposed to do."

When he returned to the kitchen, Joni asked, "Do you know anything about the flowers in the parlor?"

"What flowers?" he asked with a smile.

"I'm talking about the flower arrangement on the mantle."

"Oh, those flowers," he replied with a grin on his face. "I figured it was the least I could do to thank the lady of the house for all she's done for me this week."

"They're lovely, but you didn't have to do that."

"I owe you at least another bunch of flowers for doing my laundry. You didn't have to do that, either."

"I was doing some other things, so I just tossed them in. You wouldn't want your suitcase to set off any alarms at the airport, would you?"

A short time later, they were in the four-wheeler driving along a narrow trail up the wooded slope that led from the back of the house to the ridge. Joni was driving as if she was born in a four-wheeler. "The gas well road at the head of the hollow used to be the only way to drive up here, but I had the guy who farms for me clear this little trail. Some of my guests like to hike or ride their mountain bikes, so it makes a nice little circuit for them. The gazebo is a good place for them to stop, rest, and enjoy the view of the farm."

Ron had last climbed this slope when he and Aunt Jenny had come up here to pick blackberries. It had been a long hike, especially carrying buckets full of berries. The four-wheeler sure made life easier.

At the highest point of the ridge was a pre-manufactured gazebo with a picnic table in the center and a two-person porch swing on each side. Outside was a hand-built stone barbeque that appeared to be beyond its useful life.

"How did you get this thing up here?"

asked Ron.

"It wasn't easy, but they hauled it up the gas well road on a trailer pulled by the tractor."

"I don't remember the stone barbeque," replied Ron.

"Your uncle and a couple of his buddies built it sometime after you were here. They also built a little pavilion with a picnic table and porch swing. Your aunt and uncle used to drive up here in the jeep, spend the day, and sit together well into the night. Dad was always afraid that they'd kill themselves coming down the gas well road in the dark."

"What happened to the pavilion?"

"It rotted away and I had it removed and replaced with the gazebo a couple of years ago. I guess someone will replace this, too, one day."

Joni carried the ice chest into the gazebo and asked Ron to place her portable gas stove on the old stone barbeque. "I've got a surprise for you," she said with a smile. "Let's have our fish breakfast tonight when we have more time to enjoy it."

Ron had wondered why she had brought a portable stove and cast iron skillet on a picnic. What did he know anyway?

An hour later, they finished their old fashioned country breakfast of fried bass, fried potatoes with onions, eggs, and biscuits she had baked earlier in the day. The only thing that was different from what he remembered was the bottle of chilled white wine, most of which they polished off while preparing the rest of the meal.

The sun was setting below the treetops and the woods were beginning to darken as they finished cleaning up and loading the four-wheeler. "Let's sit in the gazebo, enjoy the evening breeze, and watch the sun go down," said Joni. "It's really peaceful up here late in the evening."

Once they were seated, Joni looked across the table and said, "I'd like to apologize for the way my grandson acted this morning. He's a good boy, but he doesn't get much discipline at home."

"He's still a kid," replied Ron. "I'm sure he'll grow out of it."

"I sure hope so. He's really talented when it comes to fixing things, especially bicycles and the like. It's too bad there's not a bicycle shop or something like that around here where he could apply those skills."

This was a line of conversation Ron didn't want to pursue any further. Instead, he said, "Speaking of boys who've apparently made good, I ran into Charlie England in town today."

"As I remember, you and Charlie weren't exactly the best of friends," she said with a smile.

"We weren't, but he stopped by while I was

eating lunch to tell me how my uncle had helped him turn his life around. He also invited me back in mid-October to go trout fishing at his camp in the mountains. Maybe I'll take him up on it if I don't have something else going on by then."

"If you do, I hope you'll also spend a few days here at the EASY REST. You've never seen how beautiful this place is when the leaves are in full color. That's when your aunt and uncle would come up here and spend the entire day until his health began to fail and the doctor made him park the jeep for good. For a couple of miss-matched characters, they were real romantics."

It was nearly dark when Joni went to the four-wheeler and came back with a small blanket. "It's getting a little chilly. Do you mind if I join you on your side of the table?"

As they sat together with the blanket over their shoulders, Ron realized that this was the first time that he had been this close to a woman since Fran had passed away. He was also beginning to feel something that he had not felt in many years. Was he falling in love with Joni again, or was this just the natural feeling a lonely man gets when he suddenly finds himself in the presence of someone who has shown him understanding and kindness? Whatever it was, he was holding back an urge to lean over and kiss her. If it was meant to be, it would happen in due time. The best thing to do now was to sit back, close his eyes, and enjoy the moment.

It was dark and the stars were out in full splendor when he opened his eyes. A quick look at his watch revealed that it was quarter past midnight. "Wake up, Joni," he said. "We must have fallen asleep. It's after midnight."

"I hope that nobody was looking for us."

"Your cell phone hasn't rung all evening, so I think we're probably safe."

They were safely at the house twenty minutes later. Joni said, "Leave the stuff in the back of the four-wheeler and I'll unload it in the morning."

"I'll unload it in the morning," replied Ron. "I don't have to leave real early."

"Then I'll have breakfast ready at the usual time. Good night!"

"Good night," he replied as he slowly made his way through the parlor to the stairs.

CHAPTER 11

Ron woke to the sound of the alarm clock. It was 7:00 a.m. and he could smell a sweet aroma from the kitchen below. He quickly put on his clothes and went downstairs only to find Joni coming through the patio door with the last of the items they had left in the four-wheeler. More and more she reminded him of Aunt Jenny.

"I told you that I'd carry those things in for you."

"Don't worry about it," she replied. "I needed something to do while the oven warms. Now go back upstairs and get ready for your trip."

Ron just sighed and went back upstairs

without another word. Why invite trouble arguing with her?

He arrived downstairs thirty minutes later with everything in hand except his overnight kit. As he arrived in the kitchen, Joni smiled and said, "Grab a cup of coffee and some granola. Everything else will be ready in about ten minutes."

It was while he was sitting there in her kitchen with his coffee that he remembered the morning he had sat at this very table and promised Uncle Fred that he would come back and go deer hunting with him during Thanksgiving break. Would he return in the fall, or would there be another fork in the road that would divert him somewhere else?

"What are you thinking about?" asked Joni as she put the muffins on the table and sat in the chair across from him.

"I was thinking about not wanting to leave."

"Why don't you stay a little longer? You're

retired and nobody else has your room reserved."

"I wish I could, but I have a meeting Monday morning with my financial advisor. I have to get all my paperwork together and fill out a retirement planning checklist before we meet."

"I thought you didn't know what you want to do."

"I don't, but at least I'll know what I can afford," he replied with a laugh. "Maybe I'll buy a place around here and find something useful to do."

"Do you really think you'd be happy here?"

"Joni, something I can't explain has already led me back here. I also don't believe the way we met again and the wonderful time we've had together this week were mere chance."

"For pity sakes, Jamie, we're as different as night and day. You're a city boy who's been around the world and I'm just a country girl who's never been out of West Virginia for more than a week at a time. Anyway, I'm pretty well tied down to this place. You're not."

"Maybe I'm meant to be tied down here, too."

"Jamie, I've also developed feelings for you, but I think it's too early to make anything of them. Maybe you should travel for awhile and sort things out before you decide where and with whom you should land. I'll still be here if we still have strong feelings for each other in October. Deal?"

"Deal."

"You'd better finish your breakfast, freshen up, and get on the road. You never know what you might encounter between here and Pittsburgh."

Ron was in the parlor a few minutes later with the rest of his belongings. After settling the bill with her, he held out his arms and asked, "Do you mind if I kiss you goodbye?"

"I wish you would, but only if you promise to come back. I'm still waiting for the postcard you promised the last time you left."

She put her arms around him and kissed him like he'd never been kissed before. Then, with tears forming in her eyes, she stepped back and said, "I wish you could stay for awhile longer."

He smiled, gave her another little kiss on the cheek, and said, "Me too, but I have to go. I'll call you when I get home and promise to send that card this time."

"You'd better," she said with a little smile on her face as he picked up his belongings and headed out the door. She didn't follow him out on the porch.

CHAPTER 12

A year had passed since his forced retirement and Ron Samuels again found himself sitting alone in his kitchen at 5:30 a.m. This time, however, he had just put a pan of bran muffins in the oven for two guests who would be up and ready for an early breakfast and departure. Joni had left Ron and Jeffrey in charge of the bed and breakfast while she, her daughter, and her granddaughter went on a three-day girls' time out in Ohio's Amish country.

Joni had left a long to-do list for the guys, but they had finished most of items the day before and planned to complete the remainder by mid-morning. That would give them the remainder of the day to uncover Uncle Fred's jeep, pull it out of the back of the barn, and inventory the parts they would need to get it running again. They planned to drive tomorrow to a junk yard in Pennsylvania where Charlie England said they could find parts for old military vehicles. For some reason, Charlie always knew where to find something, or somebody who did. If they could find what they needed, they'd be driving that old jeep around the farm again by the end of next week.

The past year had been the happiest year of Ron's life, even with all the twists and turns his whirlwind romance and marriage to Joni had taken. He and Joni had started communicating daily by phone and email the day he left, but they soon realized that they needed to be together and get to know each other. Ron had suggested coming to Floydville again before mid-October, but Joni nixed the idea fearing that it might unleash undue speculation and rumors before they were ready to announce anything.

The problem had been solved when Joni's daughter and family joined the rest of her husband's family for a week-long beach vacation in late July. Their absence from the scene had allowed Ron to discretely slip into town and spend time with Joni without anyone else knowing he had been there. The couple also spent two days and two nights together in Pittsburgh in mid-September while Joni was attending a small business seminar. It was there that Ron had officially proposed to her and she had accepted.

Ron arrived as expected in mid-October, spent the weekend fishing at Charlie's camp, and stayed the remainder of the week at the bed and breakfast. It was near the end of the week that they surprised everybody with the announcement of their engagement and plans for a December wedding at Joni's place. The ruse had worked.

The newlyweds flew to Houston the day after Christmas, leaving Jeffrey and his sister in charge of checking on the house for a negotiated fee and freedom to use of the four-wheeler in the fulfillment of their duties. They spent January travelling around southeast Texas and February staying in a beachfront condominium on South Padre Island. They then had returned to Houston to finalize the sale of his place there and drove back to West Virginia in time to get the bed and breakfast ready for guests by the first of April.

Ron came to the realization, as he sat in the quiet kitchen that morning, that his life had been a long road filled with many curves, detours, and bumps along the way. That road, however, had made a giant circle that had brought him back to the place where he always belonged. For that, he was thankful.

ABOUT THE AUTHOR

E. Randolph Underwood is a native of Salem, West Virginia, and a retired civil engineer. He lives in Martinsburg, West Virginia, with his wife Cathy. They have a daughter, Elizabeth, who currently resides with her family in California.

Mr. Underwood has also authored and self-published the following works:

Train Whistles and Other Distant Memories

Bones of Truth: Small Town Cold Case

Murder on the South Branch

The Sweater

The Property

A Road Once Travelled